W9-CND-132

For
Noah

tiger tales
5 River Road, Suite 128, Wilton, CT 06897
Published in the United States 2014
Originally published in Great Britain 2001
by Little Tiger Press
Text and illustrations copyright © 2001
Tim Warnes
Visit Tim Warnes at
www.ChapmanandWarnes.com
ISBN-13: 978-1-58925-508-1
ISBN-10: 1-58925-508-9
Printed in China
All New Materials—Polyurethane Foam
LTP/1800/0616/0513
Reg. No. PA-14954 (CN) • All rights reserved
10 9 8 7 6 5 4 3 2 1
For more insight and activities, visit us at
www.tigertalesbooks.com

Can't You Sleep, Little Puppy?

★ ★ ★

by Tim Warnes

tiger tales

Puppy couldn't sleep.
It was her first night in
her new home.

She tried sleeping
upside down.

She tried
snuggling up
with Penguin.

She even tried
lying on the
floor.

AWOOOOOOOOOOOoooo

But Puppy still
couldn't sleep.

Puppy's howling woke up Pip
the mouse. "Can't you sleep, Puppy?"
he asked. "Perhaps you should try
counting the stars like I do."

But Puppy
could only count
up to one. *That*
wasn't enough to
send her to sleep.

What could she do next?

AWOOOOOOOOOOO

Susie the bird was awake now.

"Can't you sleep, Puppy?" she twittered.

"I always have a little drink before

I go to bed."

Chirp!

Chirp!

Puppy went to her bowl
and took a drink.

Slurp!

Slurp!

But then she made a little puddle. Well, *that* didn't help! What *could* Puppy do to get to sleep?

AWOOoooooooooo

Whiskers the rabbit had woken up, too. "Can't you sleep, Puppy?" he mumbled sleepily. "I hide away in my burrow at bedtime. That always works."

Puppy dived under her blanket so that only her bottom was showing. But it was all dark under there with no light at all.

Puppy was too scared to go to sleep.

AWOOOOOOOOOOOOoooo

Flump!

Tommy the
tortoise poked
his head out
of his shell.

"Can't you sleep, Puppy?" he sighed.
"I like to sleep where it's bright
and sunny."

Plod
Plod

Puppy liked that idea . . .

. . . and turned on her flashlight!

Poor Puppy was too
tired to try anything else.

Then Tommy had a great idea . . . .

He helped Puppy into her bed.
What Puppy needed for the first
night in her new home was . . .

. . . to snuggle up with *all* her new friends.

Soon they were all fast asleep.

Good night, Puppy.